125 150 175 225
325 350 375 450
BOOKWO
W9-AYV-561
101 N UNION, SUITE 209
KENNEWICK 735-9016

KIDS CAN'T STOP READING
THE CHOOSE YOUR
OWN ADVENTURE® STORIES!

"Choose Your Own Adventure is the best thing that has come along since books themselves."
—Alysha Beyer, age 11

"I didn't read much before, but now I read my Choose Your Own Adventure books almost every night."
—Chris Brogan, age 13

"I love the control I have over what happens next."
—Kosta Efstathiou, age 17

"Choose Your Own Adventure books are so much fun to read and collect—I want them all!"
—Brendan Davin, age 11

And teachers like this series, too:
"We have read and reread, worn thin, loved, loaned, bought for others, and donated to school libraries our Choose Your Own Adventure books."

CHOOSE YOUR OWN ADVENTURE®—
AND MAKE READING MORE FUN!

Bantam Books in the Choose Your Own Adventure ® Series
Ask your bookseller for the books you have missed

VANISHED!

BY DEBORAH LERME GOODMAN

ILLUSTRATED BY FRANK BOLLE

An R.A. Montgomery Book

BANTAM BOOKS
TORONTO • NEW YORK • LONDON • SYDNEY • AUCKLAND

RL 4, IL age 10 and up

VANISHED!

A Bantam Book / September 1986

*CHOOSE YOUR OWN ADVENTURE® is a registered trademark of
Bantam Books, Inc.
Registered in U.S. Patent and Trademark Office and elsewhere.
Original conception of Edward Packard*

*All rights reserved.
Copyright © 1986 by R.A. Montgomery.
Cover art and illustrations copyright © 1986 by Bantam Books, Inc.
This book may not be reproduced in whole or in part, by
mimeograph or any other means, without permission.
For information address: Bantam Books, Inc.*

ISBN 0-553-25941-5

Published simultaneously in the United States and Canada

Bantam Books are published by Bantam Books, Inc. Its trademark, consisting of the words "Bantam Books" and the por-
trayal of a rooster, is Registered in U.S. Patent and Trademark
Office and in other countries. Marca Registrada. Bantam
Books, Inc., 666 Fifth Avenue, New York, New York 10103.

PRINTED IN THE UNITED STATES OF AMERICA

O   0 9 8 7 6 5 4 3 2 1

To Deborah Cabral

WARNING!!!

Do not read this book straight through from beginning to end. These pages contain many different adventures you may have while you search for missing persons near the Bermuda Triangle. From time to time as you read along, you will be asked to make decisions and choices. Your choices may lead to success or disaster.

The adventures you have will be the result of your own choices. After you make a choice, follow the instructions to see what happens to you next.

Beware! The Bermuda Triangle is a dangerous region where hundreds of people have mysteriously vanished.

Good luck!

"What's keeping Tony?" asks Andrea impatiently.

You finger your brand-new pilot's license as you anxiously scan the Miami airfield. As soon as Tony shows up, you're going to take your friends for a ride in your parents' small plane.

But when Tony finally arrives, his face is pale with shock. "Something happened to Jill!" he exclaims.

"What?" you gasp.

"She was sailing with her family to Eleuthera Island for Christmas, but they never got there," he explains breathlessly. "No one has heard from them since they stopped at Bimini on Thursday. The Coast Guard just announced a search."

"It's the Bermuda Triangle!" cries Andrea. "This time it's gotten Jill!"

Turn to page 2.

"What are you talking about?" you ask.

"There's a triangular area over the ocean between Miami, Puerto Rico, and Bermuda where more than a hundred boats and planes have vanished without a trace," she says.

"Oh, Andrea!" scoffs Tony. "Accidents happen all the time. That's a very heavily traveled area you're talking about."

Andrea shakes her head stubbornly. "These aren't just accidents. Boats don't normally sink in calm water within sight of land. And when planes go down, you can usually find wreckage floating nearby. I'm talking about boats and planes that have vanished into thin air! What's more, most of these disappearances take place at this time of year—between Christmas and early January."

A chill runs up your spine, but you dismiss it and say, "Look, you guys, let's argue about the Bermuda Triangle later. We should join the search for Jill."

"Great idea!" says Tony. "We can use my grandfather's boat."

"We could cover more ground if we fly," you remind him. You are eager to get behind the controls of your plane.

"We can trace her route more exactly by boat," he insists.

If you say, "You can go by boat, but Andrea and I are going by plane," turn to page 6.

If you tell him, "Okay, let's go to the marina," turn to page 36.

You continue sailing on course as the sun dips below the horizon. You're feeling discouraged that you haven't spotted anything unusual, when suddenly you notice broad stripes of underwater light about one hundred yards from the *Louisa*.

"Look!" you shout. You point out the lights to Andrea and Tony. "Let's see what they are."

"Hold on," says Andrea. "I was just about to suggest that we explore those islands over there. They look like they're part of a big coral reef. That would be a good spot for a shipwreck."

The three of you gaze through binoculars at the reef.

"The water looks pretty shallow. If we hit a sharp piece of coral, we're the ones who will end up shipwrecked," says Tony.

He turns to study the glimmering bands of white light off your side of the boat. "Those streaks sure are weird, but I don't see what they have to do with Jill's disappearance. Let's just drop the anchor and call it a day."

"Tony!" shrieks Andrea. "We can't stop now! There's still a half hour of daylight left. For all we know, Jill and her family are marooned on one of those islands!"

"Okay," he says reluctantly. "Do you want to investigate the underwater lights or the coral reef?"

If you want to get a closer look at the lights, turn to page 52.

If you want to explore the reef, turn to page 45.

4

Slowly you grope your way between palm trees toward the voices. Every now and then, you can make out a word. They are speaking English, but with a strange accent.

When you reach a small clearing, you see something that makes your hair stand on end. Three men, unlike any you've seen, are digging in the sand. They're wearing old-fashioned clothes—britches and long vests. But stranger than their clothing is the eerie light that glows around the men. They have no lanterns or torches, yet you can see them as clearly as if it were daytime.

You clutch the trunk of a tree in shock and terror as you struggle to understand what is happening. You hear the most finely dressed of the men mutter, "I know this is where I buried it! Keep digging, lads! It must be here!"

They are digging for treasure, you realize, and they are probably pirates! But why are they glowing?

Turn to page 21.

6

You and Andrea say good-bye to Tony, then walk over to your parents' plane.

"We'll duplicate Jill's path," you tell Andrea as you climb into the cockpit. "We'll fly over Bimini, then straight toward Eleuthera."

"Okay," she agrees.

Your takeoff is perfect. For an instant, your exhilaration overshadows your concern for Jill.

"We have great visibility this afternoon," says Andrea shortly after you pass Bimini. "The air is so clear."

"Except for that yellowish haze over there." You point to the south.

"A number of pilots have reported an unexplainable mist like that just before they've disappeared in the Bermuda Triangle," says Andrea.

"Then we should investigate it," you reply.

"But Jill probably wouldn't have been sailing over there," Andrea reminds you. "Besides, do you really want to fly right into a haze that has a history of devouring planes?"

You *are* nervous about flying into the yellow fog, but you can't help wondering if it has something to do with Jill's disappearance.

If you insist on investigating the haze, turn to page 8.

If you agree to continue flying directly toward Eleuthera, turn to page 85.

"I can't think of anything but food. Let's head for that small island. We can always spend the night there and paddle toward Andros Island tomorrow," you tell Andrea.

"That makes sense," replies Andrea.

But when you reach the island, you're not so sure that was a good idea. There seems to be nothing but sand and towering palm trees—no coconuts within reach, no bananas, nothing to eat.

Andrea is not discouraged. "We've barely looked around! Come on, let's check every inch of this island. I'd even eat a lizard if we found one."

Turn to page 11.

8

You radio your intention to explore the yellow mist, then head south toward Andros Island.

As you approach the fog, Andrea says, "The wings of the plane look very weird, kind of bluish green."

"That's strange," you reply uneasily. The wings of your plane are white. "Maybe it's a reflection from the water."

"I think they're beginning to glow." A note of panic creeps into Andrea's voice.

"I'm sure it's an illusion," you assure her, but goose bumps are creeping up your arms.

Gradually you realize that the entire plane is radiating light! What's more, your magnetic compass is revolving round and round. You watch with horror as the fuel gauge shoots back and forth between "full" and "empty." Your instruments are going crazy!

Turn to page 15.

You circle Eleuthera several times, but see nothing unusual.

"Well, we tried," you tell Andrea as you turn the plane toward home. "Maybe we'll spot something on our way back."

"I wouldn't want to be on a boat down there tonight. It feels like there's quite a wind." Andrea pauses, then adds, "I'm not thrilled to be in such a small plane on a windy night, either."

"Let's just hope we fly out of it," you reply.

But you don't. Even before you reach Bimini, the wind is howling against the plane, tossing it around like a toy. You've never flown in a storm, and the darkness makes it even more frightening.

"I guess we should have left Eleuthera earlier," says Andrea nervously. "I never thought about how hard it must be to navigate a plane at night."

You nod, but say nothing. Drops of sweat form on your forehead. It takes all your concentration to keep the plane on course.

"Since this isn't hurricane season, it can't be *too* bad a storm," says Andrea. "Besides, there doesn't seem to be any rain."

Suddenly a tremendous force spins the plane in a dizzying spiral. You're plunging straight toward the ocean!

"This is it!" shrieks Andrea. "The Bermuda Triangle!"

Turn to page 22.

The island is only a quarter of a mile in diameter so it doesn't take long to explore. Just as you are about to return to the raft, you step on something hard in the sand. It looks like a piece of tarnished metal.

"Hold on a minute, Andrea. Let's check this out," you say as you scoop away the sand.

You unearth an old brass chest. You hold your breath as you jiggle open the lock and lift the lid.

Gold, rubies, emeralds, and pearls! Dazzling gems and ornate jewelry! Treasure beyond your wildest dreams!

You and Andrea jump up and down, shrieking with excitement. You forget all about your growling stomach.

You try to lift the old chest, but it is much too heavy.

"One of us should stay here to guard the treasure while the other goes on to Andros Island for help," says Andrea. "Which would you rather do?"

If you volunteer to paddle to Andros Island, turn to page 79.

If you'd rather stay behind with the treasure, turn to page 81.

You strap on a parachute, then grab an inflatable life raft and wooden paddle. You swing open the door of the plane.

"Here goes!" cries Andrea, leaping into the air. She plummets for what seems an eternity before her parachute finally opens.

You glance around the plane. The control panel is still blinking madly. You close your eyes, clutch the raft and paddle, and jump.

The air rushes past you for several horrifying seconds. Whew! You finally feel the parachute unfurl behind you. As you float slowly toward the water, you prepare to inflate the life raft.

As soon as the parachute touches the waves, it becomes a heavy, soggy mess. It's hard to tread water while trying to free yourself. You splash around for a few desperate seconds before you and Andrea finally manage to untangle yourselves and inflate the raft.

The first thing Andrea says is, "Look!" She points to the sky.

A chill runs up your spine. Your plane has disappeared!

Andrea grabs the paddle and starts rowing away from the yellow haze.

Go on to the next page.

"Hold on a second," you say. "Let's figure out where we're going. Our best bet may be to head south to Andros Island. It can't be more than a few miles away."

"Through the haze?" Andrea's eyes are wide with fear. "We just jumped out of the plane to escape it. We'd be crazy to paddle right through it!"

"I don't like the idea any better than you do," you tell her, "but as far as I can recall, there's no land for miles in any other direction. We only have enough water in the survival kit to last us three or four days, and we don't have any food at all."

"We may not survive long in the yellow haze, either," says Andrea softly.

If you decide it's best to escape the menacing fog, turn to page 16.

If you want to paddle through the haze to Andros Island, turn to page 62.

"I'm calling for help," you tell Andrea, but you discover that the radio is dead.

"Turn around! Let's go home!" she pleads, shielding her eyes from the intense glare.

But you can't steer the plane! It is drawn into the menacing yellow haze and there's nothing you can do about it!

"I can't control the plane!" you shriek.

"I'm bailing out," Andrea announces. She straps on a parachute. "Where's the life raft?"

"Over there," you answer weakly.

She hands you a parachute. "Come on, let's get out of here!"

You're scared to death to stay in the plane, but you're uneasy about abandoning it in midair. You pause to think.

If you say, "Wait for me. I'm coming,"
turn to page 12.

If you tell her, "Go ahead. I'm going to see if I can get control of the plane," turn to page 80.

"Okay," you tell Andrea, "let's head north, away from the haze."

You take turns paddling. Even so, your arms and shoulders burn with each stroke of the oar. For all you know, you might be going in circles—all you can see is miles and miles of sea and sky.

As the sun sets, Andrea says, "I'm starving! I can't believe there are fish hooks in the survival kit, but no food. There's no way I'm eating a raw fish."

"At least we have a flare to signal with," you remind her. "Let's take turns sleeping and keeping watch."

You're so cold, hungry, and scared that you don't sleep much. Every small splash alarms you. You don't believe in sea monsters, but you can't help wondering what's lurking beneath the raft. By the time the sun rises, you feel awful.

But Andrea is excited. "I see an island! We're saved!"

You anxiously paddle toward it. When you reach the small island, you pull the life raft onto the beach and begin to explore.

Tall palm trees are growing everywhere. There are lots of smaller plants, too. You find a couple of bird eggs, several lizards, and a pool of fresh water, but no signs of human life.

Go on to the next page.

After refilling your water containers, you tell Andrea, "We should probably go back to the raft and start paddling again."

"Let's stay here," she suggests. "At least there's water and stuff we can eat."

"That's true," you agree, "but I think our chances of being spotted are better if we're on the water. The orange life raft and the flare are visible from the air, but this island is so lush that it would be hard for anyone to see us from above."

Yet you dread returning to the open sea.

*If you insist on going out to sea again,
turn to page 60.*

*If you prefer to stay on the island,
turn to page 88.*

Since there is no response, you figure she must be sleeping. You hurry to the place where you discovered the treasure, expecting to find Andrea napping beside the chest of jewels.

The treasure is still there, but Andrea isn't. You try to sort out all the footprints in the sand to see where she went, but they seem to go all over the place.

Even before you begin searching every inch of the island, you start to suspect that something terrible must have happened to Andrea. How could she disappear without a trace and why is the treasure still there?

After combing the island without any luck, you sadly load the treasure onto Captain Keith's boat. He is amazed by your discovery, but you're too busy wondering how Andrea vanished to care much about the fabulous gems and gleaming gold.

The End

During your second year there, you unravel some of your clothes and use the threads to create a net for catching birds and fish. You enlarge your hut and construct a stronger roof. Life becomes a little easier, but no more enjoyable. Each day is very much the same as the one before it—a boring struggle for food. You never stop hoping you'll be rescued.

On your 621st day on the island, you see a yacht approach. You and Andrea stand on the beach, shouting and waving your arms. To your relief, the people on the boat swim over to see what you're yelling about. You're finally saved!

The End

20

You hope that switching off the power was a good idea. It's pretty alarming to hear the engine grow silent while you're still in midair. You know you can coast for a while, but you're not sure how much time you have before the plane will start to descend.

The glaring light intensifies for a few seconds, then gradually fades. You immediately start up the engine again. As you turn back to Miami, you notice the yellow haze has disappeared. Suddenly, you remember Andrea. You quickly radio in a report of her evacuation, then breathe a sigh of relief. You can't believe you've survived!

As soon as you spot the Miami skyline, you know something is wrong—but what? It takes a few minutes to realize that one of the newest buildings is missing! You blink and look again. There is no mistake. This is not the same Miami you left earlier today!

You are shaking so badly you can barely land the plane. You tell yourself the building has to be there. You simply didn't see it, that's all.

But then you see something that makes your stomach lurch. The place where your parents always park their plane is already occupied—by a plane that is identical to the one you've been flying!

Turn to page 29.

And then it hits you—the men are ghosts!

You clamp your hand over your mouth to stifle your cry. Even so, the ghosts hear you whimper. They stare straight into your eyes.

"*You* stole my treasure, you bloody scoundrel!" yells the pirate leader. He stalks toward you, quivering with rage. "You'll pay! You'll pay with your life!"

You turn and run—smack into a palm tree! Before you can continue, you feel icy fingers circle your neck in a deathly grip.

A moment later, your whole body is transported to another realm where pirate feuds and searches for treasure continue endlessly. Your family and friends never find out what happened to you.

The End

You are too horrified to say anything, but you're pretty sure you're caught in a waterspout, one of the rare tornadoes that forms over water. As the wind sweeps the plane into the churning sea, you grab Andrea's hand. You don't care whether the force is supernatural or not. All that matters is knowing you're about to die.

The End

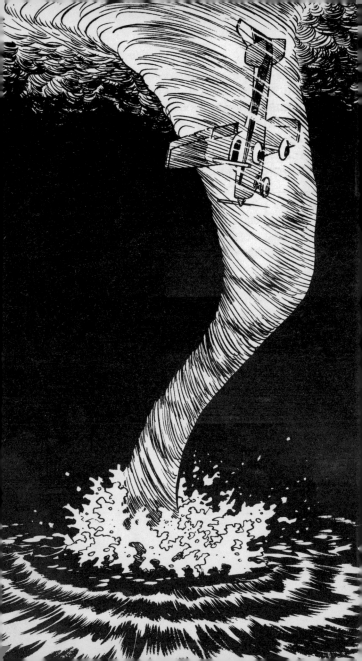

You pull the covers over your shoulders, turn your face to the wall, and shut your eyes. You try to breathe slowly, as if you are sleeping. The only trouble is, you can't stop trembling.

You freeze at the sound of heavy footsteps entering the tent. A man jabbers something urgently in a strange language. You continue breathing deeply until he shakes you impatiently.

You pretend to yawn sleepily. The guard asks you a question. Since you can't possibly answer it, you just shrug. The guard sighs with exasperation and hurries out of the tent. You're safe—at least for now.

You spend three or four hours waiting in the bed. When you finally emerge from the tent, the streets are empty.

You look around, take a deep breath, then start walking to the part of the city where you hope you'll find the transportation bubble.

The End

You hold your breath as the plane lurches forward with a sudden burst of speed. The light is so brilliant that you're tempted to cover your face, but you don't dare release the control stick. You tremble uncontrollably.

When you finally open your eyes, you find that the glow has faded. The yellow haze has disappeared. All your instruments are functioning. You slow the plane, check your location, then head for Miami.

As soon as you see Bimini, you realize something is wrong. The entire island is covered with a glittering glass dome! You become even more alarmed when you see Miami. The beaches are gone. A massive metal building rises straight out of the ocean. There's not a pool or a palm tree in sight.

"But I know this is Miami!" you exclaim with frustration. Then it hits you. It *is* Miami, but Miami of the future!

Turn to page 34.

NK525 helps you adjust to life in 2601. She teaches you to inject nutrients into your body daily, since eating food is now considered disgusting and even unhealthy. She shows you how to manage your personal robot, a temperamental machine that has trouble understanding your old-fashioned speech.

You learn that hardly any human beings live on Earth anymore, just some robot supervisors and a few scientists like NK525 who are studying the history of the planet. NK525 gets you a job as a historian. You spend all day remembering your life in the 1980s while a computer records your thoughts.

You find life in 2601 very dreary. When you complain to NK525, she says, "Maybe you would be happier on another planet or on a satellite colony. I could send you to my brother on Mars. He's one of the first pioneers there and leads a pretty exciting life. Or you could live with my sister on her satellite. She does a lot of traveling between solar systems and I bet she would take you with her sometimes."

Go on to the next page.

You shake your head. "I'd really like to return to my own time. Could I travel through another dimension back to the twentieth century?"

"Our knowledge of other dimensions is still very limited," NK525 admits. "None of our time explorers has ever returned. I'll try my best to help you, but I can't guarantee what will happen. I think you'd be much better off staying with my brother or sister."

If you're intent on returning to your own time, turn to page 32.

If you think you'd like to be a pioneer on Mars, turn to page 114.

If you decide to visit NK525's sister on a satellite, turn to page 86.

You're so confused that you just turn off the engine and leave the plane nosed against its twin. You head for home, hoping the walk will calm you.

Thank heaven your house looks pretty much as you'd expect it to look. Still, you open the door nervously, dreading what you might find.

"Hi, I'm home," you call softly.

"Who's that?" asks a strangely familiar voice.

You walk into the kitchen. There at the table, reading a magazine and eating an orange, is someone who looks exactly like you—two years ago!

You stare at each other with speechless shock.

Finally, the younger you asks, "Are you a cousin of mine, or what?"

You shake your head. "I *am* you. I'm who you'll be in about two years."

"What?" exclaims your other self. "Where did you come from?"

"I'm not sure, but I think I flew through a time warp and ended up here," you reply.

You know it's not going to be easy getting used to living with your younger self, but you tell yourself you're lucky. What would have happened if you'd traveled even further back in time, before your family existed?

The End

"We'd better not take any chances with this un-marked boat," you tell Andrea. "I think Tony is right."

"Well, let's get moving," says Tony, returning to the cabin. "We can't waste any time or it will be pitch black before we reach the debris."

As the *Louisa* sails through the darkening water, a growing sense of uneasiness grips you. You can't pinpoint what's making you nervous; you just feel as if something terrible is going to happen. You're covered with goose bumps.

Andrea is pacing the deck fretfully. When she sees you watching her, she says, "I have this creepy feeling I just can't shake."

"I know what you mean," you reply.

"Me too!" shouts Tony from the cabin.

You and Andrea go inside to join him.

"Maybe we're just afraid we'll find out that the debris is all that's left of Jill's boat," he suggests.

Andrea shakes her head. "It's more than that. I think we should drop the anchor here and start our search in the morning."

"What?" cries Tony. "I thought you were the one who was so eager to investigate the debris."

"I know," Andrea admits, blushing, "but it's getting dark so quickly that we probably won't be able to see anything. Besides, I'm just scared."

Go on to the next page.

You nod sympathetically.

"Look, we have a couple of more minutes of light," says Tony. "Let's just see if we can make it to the debris."

You know Tony's suggestion makes sense, but it's hard to ignore the sense of doom you feel.

If you agree to continue toward the debris, turn to page 39.

If you insist on stopping for the night, turn to page 96.

"I don't care what happens, I just want to go home," you tell NK525.

"All right," she says. On her computer, she locates what she calls a "dimensional passage." To you it's just the familiar yellow haze. "It's floating just south of Bermuda," she tells you. "You can fly there in my spare rocket and I'll donate your plane to our museum."

"No, I'll go in my own plane," you insist. "I don't feel comfortable driving your rockets and the last thing I need now is an accident."

You thank NK525 and say good-bye. You know you'll miss her.

It's easy to find the yellow haze. As you fly into it, the plane glows and the control panel goes wild, just as before. You sit back, close your eyes, and give the engine all the fuel you can. You feel every bit as terrified as you did last time.

As soon as you emerge into the new time, you fly back to Miami. The vast building you saw in 2601 is still there, but the roof is gutted with holes. You land the plane and try to find someone who can tell you what year it is. There is no one in sight, not even a robot.

With sickening horror, you fly north to search for signs of life, but you soon run out of gas and are forced to land.

It is the year 3817 and you are the only human being on Earth.

The End

"Let's just make sure no one on that yacht is in trouble," you reply. "It will only take a minute. Then we can head toward the debris."

"You go on board if you want, but I'm staying right here," says Tony. "Be careful!"

You and Andrea climb onto the yacht. It is by far the largest boat you've ever set foot on.

"I'll investigate the cabin and you check below the deck," you tell Andrea.

"Okay. We'll meet back here," she replies.

Carefully, quietly, you enter the galley. No one is there, but you find plenty of food. There are dirty paper plates in the trash.

You tiptoe into a bedroom. What a mess! Clothing, towels, and magazines are strewn all over the room. You notice a wallet lying under a pack of cigarettes. Maybe it's a clue!

Just as you stoop to pick up the wallet, you hear Andrea scream from below the deck. You freeze. Your whole body is trembling. You don't know what to do.

Should you try to help Andrea yourself or sneak back to the *Louisa* to call the Coast Guard?

If you decide to go below the deck alone, turn to page 40.

If you think it's best to get back to the Louisa, *turn to page 87.*

34

You land your plane on the roof of the building. As you climb out of the cockpit, a small crowd of robots and a few human beings rush toward you. Mustering all your courage, you extend your hand to one of the women.

She shakes your hand and tells you her name is NK525. "You're from the twentieth century, aren't you?" she asks, eyeing your plane.

You nod, dumbfounded, and she continues, "Don't be alarmed. You must have flown through another dimension into our time."

"What *is* your time?" you ask fearfully.

"2601," answers one of the robots in monotone.

Turn to page 26.

On the way to the harbor, you stop off at your house to tell your parents you'll be spending a few days on Tony's boat. You grab some food, then join Andrea and Tony in the car. You drive to the marina where Tony's grandfather moors the *Louisa,* his thirty-foot boat.

The *Louisa* cruises out of Biscayne Bay toward Bimini. You and Andrea scan the horizon through binoculars while Tony steers and listens to the radio reports.

The hours pass uneventfully. Toward dusk, Tony emerges from the cabin and says, "A plane spotted some debris not too far north of here."

"Let's check it out!" cries Andrea eagerly.

"I don't think that's a good idea," says Tony. "My grandfather wouldn't want me taking his boat there, especially after dark. Sometimes there are pirates in that area."

"Pirates? In the twentieth century?" you ask with astonishment.

"Sure," Tony answers. "They're not like you read about in stories. They're regular crooks who steal boats—but they're just as dangerous as the old-fashioned pirates used to be."

Go on to the next page.

Andrea snorts in disbelief. "This isn't a pleasure cruise. We have to act quickly and we have to take chances. The debris may be gone by tomorrow morning."

Tony digs his hands into his pockets and stares at the deck. Then he glances at you and asks, "What do you think we should do?"

If you say, "We'd better forget about the debris," turn to page 3.

If you tell him, "Let's take a look at the debris," turn to page 74.

"I don't know what happened to my friends," you lie. "I fell asleep and when I woke up, they were gone."

The Coast Guard brings you back to Miami where the questioning begins. The police even give you a lie detector test, which you fail. Time and time again, you tell your false story. Even though no one believes you, the case is finally closed for lack of evidence.

The worst part is insisting to your friends' families that you don't know what happened to Andrea and Tony. For months afterward, you feel nervous whenever you see them.

After lying about Tony and Andrea's disappearance so many times, you almost come to believe the tale yourself. You lie awake at night wondering if your friends really did travel to the planet Vaena, or was it all a crazy dream?

The End

"Let's keep going," you reply, trying to dismiss your unexplainable fear. "I'll go out to the deck and look for debris."

Andrea follows you. You raise your binoculars to your eyes and scan the horizon. Your hands are trembling.

"I can't see anything," says Andrea. "I hope Tony is going in the right direction."

By the time darkness falls, you feel even more uneasy. Except for a sprinkling of stars and a slender crescent of moon, you're surrounded by vast blackness. *Anything* could be out there waiting for you.

"Let's call it a day," Tony announces, shutting off the engine.

You are just about to dig out the sandwiches you brought for dinner when you feel the boat lurch.

"What was that?" you shout. You realize that the water is getting rough. It's so rough you have to hold on to the sides of the boat to keep your balance.

"I don't know!" Tony yells. "These giant waves just came out of nowhere!"

"And they're getting worse!" cries Andrea.

Turn to page 46.

Not caring how much noise you make, you race to the stairway leading under the deck. All you can think about is helping Andrea.

You've bolted down three steps when two muscular blond men grab you.

"Let go of me!" you yell before one covers your mouth. You bite his hand and scream, "HELP!" but moments later, you find yourself bound and gagged. From the corner of your eye, you see Andrea tied up across the room.

Just then, you hear footsteps above you. Tony runs down the stairs, only to be grabbed by the two men. Your heart sinks.

"Anyone else on your boat?" one of the men asks you.

You're so scared you can barely shake your head.

"All right, Mickey!" laughs the man. "We got ourselves another boat!"

"Nice job, Shark," replies Mickey. "You take care of bringing their boat in and I'll meet you tomorrow night at Keller's Point."

Shark nods and hurries up the stairs.

Turn to page 44.

You barely fit in the basket. You tuck your head to your knees and hold your breath.

Someone enters the tent. Your heart is beating so loudly that you're sure it will give you away. You try to stay perfectly still even though the dried sea-weed feels very prickly.

The footsteps come closer. You cringe. This is it, you tell yourself, I've had it. But to your surprise, you hear the heavy thud of boots heading out of the tent. The shouts of your pursuers fade as they hurry down the street.

How lucky you are! Deciding to continue to-ward the transportation bubble, you start to scramble out of the tall basket. To your horror, the basket tips. You fall against the membranous wall, tearing it, and land in a heap on the street outside the tent. An alarmed passerby quickly calls the search party.

Before you can even stand up, the guards sur-round you. "You fool," cries the fish woman. "You'll be punished with death."

The End

You try to calm yourself so you can think. Mickey and Shark seem too handsome to be pirates, yet you know they're dangerous. You realize there's a good chance they might even kill you. You wonder if there's any way you can stall for time. What if you suggest they demand a ransom for you? After all, the money might tempt the pirates, and it would offer you a chance of survival. You remember reading that the success rate for catching kidnappers is fairly high.

On the other hand, you don't *know* that the men plan to kill you. But you do know that your parents couldn't afford to pay a high ransom. You might even endanger yourself by speaking up. Maybe if you just behave, the pirates won't hurt you.

If you're intent on persuading Mickey to hold you for ransom, turn to page 55.

If you think good behavior is the key to your survival, turn to page 97.

"I'd like to check out the coral reef," you reply.

"Okay," says Tony, "but we'll have to be very careful or I could ruin the boat."

He directs the *Louisa* through a narrow inlet between two tiny islands.

"These are hardly bigger than sandbars!" says Tony. "I don't know what you expect to find here. We'd be able to see Jill's boat if it were stuck on this reef."

Just as you begin to think he's right, Andrea shouts, "Look!"

You turn to see HELP! written in the sand!

"They must be here!" you gasp.

"Anyone could have written that," says Tony in a maddeningly reasonable voice. "In fact, it's probably a joke. I don't see any footprints in the sand."

Andrea rolls her eyes. "It doesn't matter *who* wrote that message—we can't ignore it!"

Turn to page 54.

The *Louisa* bounces up and down, tossing you and your friends across the deck.

"I'll get the life vests," you shout as you grope your way to the chest where they are stored.

You hear Tony mutter, "It's not a whirlpool. Could it be a seiche?"

"A what?"

"An enormous wave caused by an underwater earthquake," he answers.

You start to open the chest, but your fingers are yanked away. The *Louisa* flips on her side, hurling you, Tony, and Andrea into the dark water. You choke and sputter as you struggle to the surface. Suddenly, the edge of the boat crashes through your skull, plunging you into black nothingness. The seiche carries your body so far into the ocean that no one is ever able to find it.

The End

48

The beings carry each of you to separate rooms in the alien ship. After the door to your room automatically seals itself into the wall, your captors let go of you. Your eyes dart around in search of an escape route, but there's no place you can go. You turn to face the beings. They're wearing some kind of breathing device so you can't see much of their faces. You're scared out of your wits!

You hear a soft voice—not through your ears, but somewhere inside your head—say, "Don't be frightened. We won't hurt you."

"Wh-who are you?" you stammer aloud.

"We're from Vaena, a magnificent planet in a distant solar system," says the voice in your brain. "We're doing research about Earth and we'd like to bring you back to Vaena. Will you come?"

"Do I have a choice?"

"Certainly. If you are unwilling to assist us, we will give you a medicine to erase your memory of the last hour. We will then return you and your boat to the surface."

"What about Andrea and Tony?" you ask. "What will happen to them?"

"Each of you must decide individually," says the voice. "Please consider carefully, and remember, we will never harm you."

Turn to page 56.

You fake a swallow, then pretend you're falling asleep. You let yourself collapse on the floor.

The extraterrestrials carry you back to the *Louisa* and place you on the deck. You hear them leave, and feel the spacecraft release its grip on the boat.

In case the beings from Vaena are watching, you lie on the deck for a while. You try to remember every detail of your experience.

Suddenly, you feel the boat rock. You hear a loud whirring. You open your eyes just in time to see the spacecraft whirl into the sky. You realize sadly that you'll never see Tony and Andrea again.

When the spaceship has vanished, you stand up and stretch. Since you have no idea how to sail home, you try to figure out how the radio works so you can call for help.

"This is the *Louisa* calling," you announce. "I'm somewhere west of Bimini and I need help. My two friends have disappeared and I don't know how to get back to Miami."

"What happened to the other people aboard?" asks the radio controller.

You hesitate. You know people will think you're crazy if you tell them about the beings from Vaena, but what else can you say? How will you ever explain all this to Andrea and Tony's parents?

If you decide to tell the truth, turn to page 57.

If you think it will be easier to pretend you don't know what happened, turn to page 38.

"You won't regret your decision to come to Vaena," an extraterrestrial tells you. "Your companions have also agreed to join us. They're eager to visit another planet and have new experiences."

"Did you capture my other friend, Jill, and her family as well?" you ask.

The Vaenatians look confused. "You are the first human beings we have collected for several months," says one. "Now follow us. We'll prepare you for the journey to Vaena."

During most of the flight, you, Andrea, and Tony sleep with electrodes attached to your scalps. As you rest, you absorb all kinds of information about the Vaenatian language and culture.

"If everything we learned is true, Vaena is really going to be a wonderful place to live!" you exclaim to your friends as the spacecraft lands.

Turn to page 59.

Eventually, you become a prominent teacher of interplanetary culture. Your studies of other inhabited planets make you realize how vastly superior Vaenatian civilization is to all others. You feel fortunate to be able to live here.

One day, a Vaenatian leader offers you a special challenge. "We're worried about your native planet, Earth," she tells you. "Each year, human beings become more selfish and aggressive. We expect a nuclear war to erupt there very soon."

"Is there anything we can do to save Earth?" you ask. You can hardly imagine your native planet blasted to dust.

"We're hoping to convert Earthlings to a more cooperative and peaceful way of life—the Vaenatian way of life," the leader tells you. "By changing their ways, we may be able to prevent a war. We need dedicated missionaries, former Earthlings, for the job. Are you interested?"

At first, the idea of seeing your family and friends again thrills you. What's more, you can't think of anything more important than preventing the destruction of Earth. But then you realize what an enormous task it is. You remember how quickly most human beings reject new ideas. How could you ever persuade them to change all their values? You're not sure you want to leave your happy life on Vaena for a mission that may very well fail.

*If you finally decide it's worth a try,
turn to page 61.*

If you turn down the offer, turn to page 115.

"Let's see what's making the water glow," you say.

You sail to the middle of a wide band of light. As you peer over the side of the boat, Andrea says, "Astronauts have reported seeing lights like this in the water here. I wonder if it has anything to do with ships that disappear in the Bermuda Triangle."

Tony rolls his eyes. You're too busy studying the light to pay attention.

"Something is moving down there and it's not just fish!" you cry. "It looks metallic." The three of you gaze intently into the water.

"It's coming toward us!" shouts Andrea.

You watch with speechless horror as an enormous bowl-shaped spaceship rises up beneath you, completely surrounding the *Louisa*. A glowing dome closes over you. Mechanical arms seize the boat. Before you know what is happening, a crowd of strange, tall beings with pale yellow skin grab you, Tony, and Andrea. You struggle to get away, but the webbed hands grip you with inhuman power.

Turn to page 48.

Tony silently guides the boat through a network of shallow channels. To your disappointment, you spot no signs of life. Maybe the message *was* just a joke.

"We can't go any further," Tony finally insists. "The water is just too shallow."

"There are still so many islands we haven't checked!" wails Andrea with frustration.

"Why don't we leave the boat here and explore by foot?" you suggest. "We could easily swim between the islands."

Tony shakes his head. "We should get the boat out of here while it's still light out. This is going to be very tricky."

You understand his concern, but you hate to leave without investigating the remaining islands.

*If you agree to sail out of the reef,
turn to page 64.*

*If you're intent on completing the search,
turn to page 78.*

First, you'll have to get Mickey's attention. You grunt softly until he glances at you, then jerk your head, signaling him to come closer.

But it doesn't work. Mickey just laughs and says, "I know those gags are uncomfortable, but you'll have to get used to them."

You shake your head and continue making noises.

Finally, Mickey asks, "Got something to say?"

You nod eagerly.

He reaches into his sweatshirt and pulls out a gun. "All right," says Mickey, "Tell me what you have to, but no funny business."

You feel him press the cool metal of the gun against your scalp. He loosens the rags tied around your head and removes the towel stuffed inside your mouth.

"Are you going to kill us?" you blurt out.

One half of his mouth curls up in a lazy, lopsided grin. "That's for me to know, kid."

"Why don't you kidnap us?" you suggest.

"I'm a pirate, not a kidnapper." Mickey spits on the floor.

"Our parents are rich," you insist. "They would pay a gigantic ransom." You dare not look at your friends' reactions to this outrageous lie.

"Rich?" asks Mickey. "How rich?"

"Millionaires," you assure him.

"Let me think about it," says Mickey. "Give me your names and phone numbers."

He scribbles the information on the back of his hand, then binds the rags around your head again.

Turn to page 113.

"If I go with you, how long will I stay?"

"You must stay with us forever, but we assure you that once you see the beauty of Vaena and recognize the superiority of our civilization, you will never miss Earth or your family."

You're incredibly curious about Vaena. You know this is the chance of a lifetime, but you can't believe you won't miss your family and friends. And what if Vaena isn't so wonderful?

If you say, "All right, I'll stay with you," turn to page 50.

If you tell them, "I'm sorry, but I want to stay on Earth," turn to page 91.

"My friends have gone to the planet Vaena with some extraterrestrials," you reply sheepishly.

To your relief, the radio controller doesn't burst into laughter. He questions you very slowly and patiently about your location. But when the Coast Guard finally arrives, you find they have brought along a straitjacket and a psychiatrist!

At first, everyone thinks you're crazy. But you stick to your story, and gradually people start to believe you. Experts from NASA and the CIA question you. You're invited to the White House to meet the President. You appear on the six o'clock news.

Turn to page 76.

Seconds before the doors open, the Vaenatians remove their breathing devices. To your disappointment, it's your turn to put on respiratory masks. You feel awkward and embarrassed, knowing it makes you look like a cross between an elephant and a giant insect.

But you forget your embarrassment as soon as you step out of the spacecraft. Throngs of Vaenatians welcome you with a strange but comforting cooing sound. You're dazzled by light. Everything glows with a muted iridescence.

"It's beautiful!" whispers Andrea.

Tony is not so sure. "Look!" he exclaims. "The sky is violet!"

You're surprised by the absence of buildings. You remind yourself that Vaenatian weather is always mild and there is no such thing as snow or rain, but you imagined they would have houses for privacy.

However, the Vaenatians treat you—and each other—with exceptional kindness and respect, and within months, you feel completely at home. You miss your family and friends on Earth, but you love your new planet.

Turn to page 51.

"Andrea, no one will ever find us if we stay on this island," you say. "I don't like floating any better than you do, but believe me, no one can rescue us if they don't *see* us."

"I hope you're right," she replies.

"Let's drink some more water, then go get the raft."

As you paddle away from the island, you try to be cheerful. "I can feel gallons of water sloshing around in my stomach," you say. "At least we won't die of thirst right away."

"Right," she answers, "we may even lose a few extra pounds. And heaven knows we're getting terrific suntans."

"Just imagine the story we'll have to tell when we get back to school," you add.

Andrea's smile disappears. "*If* we get back," she solemnly reminds you. Suddenly, you don't feel so lighthearted.

Turn to page 71.

"I accept the challenge," you tell the Vaenatian leader. "I'll return to Earth as a missionary."

Your journey begins a few days later. Several other former Earthlings accompany you, but Andrea and Tony have chosen to remain on Vaena. On the way, you calculate that nearly seven Earth years have passed since you left your home.

You decide it's best to start by converting your own family, so you get off the spacecraft at Miami. You head straight for your house.

It's Sunday. Your parents are reading the newspaper when you ring the doorbell.

"Mom? Dad? It's me," you say when they come to the door.

They recognize you immediately. At first, you hug each other and everyone cries a little. But soon enough, your mother asks, "Whatever happened to you? We thought you drowned!"

Turn to page 72.

"Listen, Andrea, we're better off going south where we know there's land," you say. "Besides, we don't know that the yellow fog is dangerous. Maybe there was something wrong with the plane."

"You don't believe that," says Andrea. And she's right, you're terrified of traveling through the haze.

Nonetheless, you take the paddle and begin rowing toward Andros Island. When your shoulders start to ache, Andrea relieves you. You take turns rowing all through the night.

By morning, the mysterious yellow haze has vanished. But you are discouraged to find that Andros Island still appears to be several miles away.

"I've never been so hungry in my life!" groans Andrea.

"Me neither!" you reply.

You know there isn't any point in complaining though, so you just keep paddling away.

Go on to the next page.

After a couple of hours, you spot a small island about half a mile to the west. As far as you can tell, it is uninhabited.

"Want to head for that island?" you ask Andrea. "Maybe we could find something to eat there."

"I don't know," she answers. "If we keep on going, we may be able to reach Andros Island by sundown. I dread the thought of spending another night on this raft."

You are eager to get to safety as soon as possible, but you're also ravenous. At this point, you can even imagine eating insects!

If you want to go to the small island, turn to page 7.

If you decide to ignore your pangs of hunger and continue to Andros Island, turn to page 83.

Tony begins to edge the boat around.

Andrea peers over the side and says, "There are all kinds of scraggly coral branches poking up."

Tony grimaces. "You wouldn't *believe* how sharp the coral is. We're going to have a heck of a time getting out of here in one piece."

Slowly, the *Louisa* cruises through the treacherous inlets. You are almost out of the reef when you hear an awful scratching noise on the bottom of the boat.

"Is that coral?" you ask, dreading the answer.

Tony nods grimly. "We're through the worst of it. We just have to keep . . ."

But a terrible ripping noise interrupts him. Coral tears apart the hull of the *Louisa* and water floods into the boat!

"Oh, no!" wails Tony, covering his face with his hands.

"Quick!" you shout. "Radio for help or we'll be stranded here!"

As Tony calls the Coast Guard, you and Andrea climb off the boat and begin swimming toward the nearest island. The *Louisa* is ruined and your search for Jill is over.

The End

You fly the plane in a wide curve as you turn back toward Miami. "I'll fly a few degrees north of our original route so we can check out some new territory," you say.

"Good idea," says Andrea. She gazes down at the glittering sea.

After just a few minutes of flying, she says, "I think I see something—a yellow life raft!"

"You're kidding!" You quickly take a look. Sure enough, there's a spot of yellow floating in the water. It seems too small to be a boat.

"Can we get a closer look?" asks Andrea.

You circle around at a lower altitude. The closer you get, the more convinced you are that the yellow shape is a life raft. You can even see four people in it.

"We've found them!" you exclaim, nearly exploding with joy.

"Not necessarily," warns Andrea. "We've found some people, but we can't be sure they are Jill's family."

"Oh, Andrea!" you scoff. "How many shipwrecks do you think take place here?"

"A lot," she replies. "That's one reason why people don't take the Bermuda Triangle seriously. They say this is a heavily traveled, unpredictable area of water and accidents are bound to happen."

Go on to the next page.

You don't reply. Instead you radio in a report of your sighting and begin circling even lower.

"Well, we saved *somebody*," says Andrea.

"Look," you say, struggling to see better, "one of them is wearing a red jacket like Jill's."

"Maybe so, but they all look too blond to be Jill's family," Andrea replies.

The suspense is killing you! Even though it's not wise to fly any closer to the water, you're dying to see if it's Jill's family in the raft.

*If you decide to risk a closer look,
turn to page 100.*

*If you think it's better to let the Coast Guard
find out, turn to page 105.*

You race down an unfamiliar street. Someone darts out of a doorway and grabs your arm, but you yank yourself free. Then you run even faster, for you finally see the transportation bubble. It's no longer attached to the *Louisa*.

It is not until you leap inside that you realize you don't know how to drive the bubble. The words on the controls are not in English. There is no time to study the many switches and dials. You frantically grope around until you hear the motor begin to hum. And not a moment too soon—the crowd is just yards away!

The bubble begins to rise inside the walls of the city. The fish people shriek below. You feel a sudden thud as the bubble hits the huge ceiling that keeps the water out. The bubble breaks through the membrane, floating into the ocean above. You watch with shock as water rushes into the gaping hole, crushing the fish-skin tents and drowning all the inhabitants. A lump forms in the back of your throat. You realize Andrea and Tony are doomed.

Within minutes, the bubble reaches the surface of the water and bumps into something else. To your relief, you find it's a giant ocean liner. The crew hauls the peculiar bubble aboard. You climb out of it, take a deep breath, and slowly begin to explain what happened. You still can't believe you really managed to escape.

The End

For the next few hours, you hardly talk. You continue paddling and staring at the vast blueness that surrounds you.

And then you see it—a shimmering speck in the sky!

"Andrea! There's a plane! It's flying toward us!"

"Wave your arms! Shout! We have to get their attention!" she yells frantically.

You don't bother to remind her that the pilot can't possibly hear your screams. Instead, you quickly send up the flare.

But the plane continues past you.

"I don't believe it!" wails Andrea, fighting back tears.

"Look!" you exclaim. "They're circling back!"

You wave your arms desperately as the plane soars around you three times.

"They must have seen us," you tell Andrea. "Surely they've called for help."

In less than an hour, you and Andrea are sailing home on a Coast Guard ship.

The End

"Well," you reply, "it's a long story. Andrea, Tony, and I were transported to a wonderful far-away planet called Vaena."

Your parents eye each other nervously.

"I'm serious," you insist. "It's a remarkable place. In fact, I've returned here to persuade Earthlings to start living more like Vaenatians. If only human beings would stop thinking in terms of separate nations and start recognizing the importance of planetary concerns. . . ."

Your father moans. "It's a cult. These Vaenatians are really just a crazy cult, aren't they?"

"No!" you exclaim.

Your mother begins to cry. "Our child is mentally ill!"

"Totally insane!" adds your father.

You end up seeing countless psychiatrists. You cling to the truth so persistently that before long, everyone is convinced you've lost your mind. Your parents sadly commit you to a mental asylum where you spend the rest of your life dreaming of the planet Vaena. You never learn what became of the other missionaries.

The End

As mayor, you discover you have a real talent for governing. You treat everyone in the city fairly and people respect you. New Miami flourishes under your leadership. You become governor, and finally president of the entire planet.

Except for occasional vacations on Jupiter, you spend the rest of your life on Mars. You never return to Earth, even for a brief visit. But sometimes when you recognize your former planet glowing among the stars in the night sky, you find yourself wondering what would have happened to you if you'd stayed in the twentieth century. You can't believe you could be any happier than you are now.

The End

As the *Louisa* cruises north, you think about the reported debris. You keep hoping it won't be the remains of Jill's boat. You remind yourself it could be almost anything—garbage, old driftwood, the wreckage from someone else's boat.

You've sailed just a few knots when you notice a handsome yacht floating perfectly still in the middle of an endless stretch of water.

"There's something strange about that boat," says Tony.

"No lights and no people on deck," you comment.

"And look," says Andrea, "no name or numbers. Aren't all boats supposed to have some numbers, sort of like a license plate?"

Tony nods.

"Maybe they're in trouble. Let's get a closer look," you suggest.

Tony pulls the *Louisa* alongside the unmarked yacht.

"Hello! Hello! Are you all right?" you shout.

There is no answer. You shiver, remembering tales of ghost ships.

"Let's go aboard," says Andrea.

"Are you kidding?" Tony exclaims. "That yacht could be a pirate's decoy. As soon as we step on the boat, they could grab us and steal the *Louisa*."

Go on to the next page.

You and Andrea eye each other. You're all too familiar with Tony's cautiousness.

"Tony, there may be people on board who need our help," Andrea insists.

"Then why didn't they answer when we called?" he challenges her.

"Maybe they *can't* answer. Maybe they're hurt," says Andrea. "We should really check this out."

"Please don't," pleads Tony. "And besides, what about the debris you wanted to investigate?"

Andrea backs down. "That's right," she says. She turns to you and asks, "What do you think we should do?"

If you want to ignore the yacht and continue toward the debris, turn to page 30.

If you decide to board the unmarked boat, turn to page 33.

One night, soon after the government launches a major investigation into underwater spacecraft, you are abruptly wakened from your sleep. A webbed hand is clamped over your mouth. Six beings from Vaena carry you out of your house and into a blinking circular spaceship. The door slides shut.

As soon as they release you, you scream and tear at the door. Inside your head, a voice says, "We asked you to cooperate. We were fair, but you tricked us. We must remove you from Earth before you cause any more harm to our research."

You feel the spacecraft rise through the air. "Are you taking me to Vaena?" you ask.

"Oh, no," says the voice. "We can't have untrustworthy types like you on Vaena. We will bring you to Malanka, the prison planet."

You never find out if Vaena is as wonderful as its inhabitants believe. But you do learn one thing— in every way, Malanka is a thousand times worse than Earth.

The End

"Stay here with the boat," you tell Tony. "Andrea and I will just check those last few islands."

Tony frowns. "Okay, but hurry. And be careful not to touch any coral—it's really sharp!"

You and Andrea quickly change into swimsuits and jump into the water. You alternately swim and walk to the most distant cluster of islands.

After a brief look around, Andrea says, "It's getting dark. We'd better head back to the boat."

You start to turn, but a flash of orange from another small island catches your eye. You pause to study the spot of bright color.

"Andrea, what do you think that could be?" you ask, pointing to the orange shape.

"Let's go see," she suggests.

Turn to page 112.

"You can stay here with the treasure," you tell Andrea.

Even though you're still hungry and thirsty, the discovery of treasure makes you feel much better. You say good-bye to Andrea and cheerfully set off for Andros Island.

But without anyone to take turns paddling, your progress is slow. You row all through the night. By daybreak, you find yourself floating alongside a small fishing boat.

"Help!" you shout. "Help!"

A wizened old man hauls you aboard. "Captain Keith's the name," he tells you as he wraps a blanket around you. You introduce yourself and ask if he will take you back to the island where Andrea is waiting.

"Sure 'nough, mate," says Captain Keith. "Let's go!"

As you cruise toward the small island, he tells you pirate tales, but you're only half listening. The other part of you is fantasizing about the treasure.

Captain Keith drops the anchor near the island and you paddle to shore in the life raft. "Andrea!" you shout. "Andrea, I'm here!"

Turn to page 18.

"Good luck!" you call to Andrea as she plummets from the plane. You have a dreadful feeling you'll need more luck than she will.

The controls are still spinning and flashing erratically. There is nothing from the radio, not even the crackle of static. When you look out the windows, you see something new—the wings look fuzzy, as if they're dissolving!

"What should I do?" you scream.

You wonder if you could break free of this nameless force by suddenly accelerating the plane. Or what would happen if you cut off all power to the engine? As you turn your eyes away from the blinding light, it occurs to you that anything you do might make matters worse!

If you close the throttle, cut off the fuel supply, and turn off the ignition, turn to page 20.

If you accelerate the plane, turn to page 25.

If you sit back and just hope for the best, turn to page 109.

"If you're sure you don't mind going for help, I'd just as soon stay here," you tell Andrea.

You walk her back to the life raft, then wave good-bye as Andrea slowly paddles away. When you can no longer see the orange raft, you return to the trunk of jewels. You'd like to examine the treasure, but you're unbearably tired. You curl up beside the chest and tell yourself you'll have plenty of time to sift through the jewels later. After all, it will take Andrea many hours to reach Andros Island. You quickly fall asleep.

When you wake up, it is so dark you can't see anything but the stars and a thin sliver of the moon. You start to drift back to sleep, but then you hear something—voices coming from the other side of the island!

It must be Andrea with the Coast Guard, you joyfully tell yourself. Since they surely have flashlights, you decide to stay right where you are.

But after waiting nearly an hour, you begin to wonder why they haven't located you by now. You are just about to begin shouting, when you suddenly realize the voices may not belong to Andrea and the Coast Guard. A chill runs up your spine. Who else could it be?

You're tempted to go find out, but you're also worried about leaving the treasure unguarded.

If you try to get a glimpse of whoever has come to the island, turn to page 4.

If you're determined to stay with the treasure, turn to page 94.

"Okay, let's keep going," you tell Andrea. You are determined not to think about your hunger or thirst.

You stare intently at Andros Island as you paddle toward it. The glare of the sun on the waves is giving you a headache and you feel weaker with every minute that passes.

Suddenly, a snakelike form slithers into the raft. Before you know what's happening, two more of them are writhing around you.

"It's an octopus!" screams Andrea.

You try to beat the groping arms away with the oar, but three more tentacles quickly grip the raft. With one big swoosh the raft flips over, dumping you and Andrea into the creature's flailing arms.

As you struggle to free yourself, you catch sight of the sea monster's body. It isn't an octopus after all, but a giant squid with ten powerful arms that cling to your legs, wrists, and finally your face. You see Andrea break away from the creature, but there is no hope for you. The giant squid drags you deeper and deeper into the sea, then slowly draws your body into its gaping mouth.

The End

The pink pill takes effect immediately. You yawn and yawn. You can't keep your eyes open. Before you know what is happening, you crumple to the ground, asleep.

You wake up on the deck of the *Louisa*.

"Tony? Andrea?" you murmur. "Why did you let me fall asleep?"

There is no answer. In fact, as you anxiously look around, you realize your friends are nowhere to be seen! What could have happened to them? And why didn't it happen to you, too?

You search all over the boat. You look overboard. Your heart does a frenzied tap dance in your chest. You've never felt so alone in your entire life.

As you stare at the endless darkness of sea and sky, you can't help thinking of everything Andrea said about the Bermuda Triangle.

The End

"I guess we'd better stay on course and forget about the yellow mist," you tell Andrea. You continue flying toward Eleuthera but see no signs of a shipwreck or anything that resembles Jill's boat.

"The sun is going down," says Andrea. "Shouldn't we be heading home? Maybe we'll see something we missed on the way out."

"Let's just circle the island a few times," you suggest.

Andrea glances nervously at the position of the sun. "Unless we head back to Miami right away, it will be dark before we're even halfway there. Are you sure you're experienced enough to fly at night?"

You have to admit that flying in darkness makes you uneasy, but you'd really like to do a thorough search of the Eleuthera shoreline before you leave.

If you say, "Let's just take a few spins around the island before we leave," turn to page 9.

If you tell Andrea, "You're right. We'd probably better not fly home after sundown," turn to page 66.

"I'd like to visit a satellite colony," you tell NK525.

"Good!" she replies. "We'll go to my sister's tomorrow."

It takes just a few hours to fly to the satellite where EE721, NK525's sister, lives. Before you enter the huge metallic structure that houses hundreds of people, you gaze back at Earth. You wonder if you'll ever set foot on your native planet again.

EE721 hugs her sister and welcomes you into her spacious apartment. It contains no furniture, only a luxurious rug and dozens of silky pillows. One wall is covered with computer screens, keyboards, and hundreds of switches, buttons, and dials. A row of eleven towering androids stands along another wall, awaiting orders from EE721. You're not sure why, but you find these massive robots very unnerving.

The two sisters chat for hours while you grow bored and sleepy. Finally, EE721 says, "Let's go for a jog around the satellite corridor."

NK525 eagerly agrees, but you're too tired. "I'll wait here," you reply.

"Fine," says EE721. "Just don't touch any of the robot controls on the wall. We'll be back in an hour or so."

Turn to page 93.

You hurry out of the bedroom, through the galley, and out to the deck as quietly as you can. You see Tony waiting anxiously on the *Louisa*. He helps you aboard and asks, "Was that Andrea screaming? What happened? Where is she?"

"I don't know," you reply breathlessly. "Just call the Coast Guard and move away from that yacht."

While Tony races into the cabin to start up the engine, you remain on deck to keep an eye on the other boat. You're worried about Andrea.

"The Coast Guard will be here in fifteen or twenty minutes," Tony tells you.

"Fifteen or twenty!" you echo. It sounds like forever!

Turn to page 99.

"You're right," you tell Andrea. "Let's stay on the island. We can leave the orange raft on the beach where there aren't any trees. Someone flying overhead is sure to see it."

"Good idea," she replies. "Now try to remember everything Robinson Crusoe did to survive on his island."

First you build a small hut out of driftwood and palm fronds. It collapses during the night. You construct seven more shelters before you build one that's sturdy enough to withstand the steady winds.

Meanwhile, there's also food to think about. With the fish hooks in your survival kit, you're able to catch fish. You also eat leaves and lizards. Every now and then, you have a special treat when a coconut falls to the ground. You spend a lot of time dreaming about chocolate chip cookies and Thanksgiving dinners.

Each day, you cut a notch into the bark of a tree that serves as your calendar. First your birthday passes, then Andrea's, and before you know it, you've spent one full year on the island.

Turn to page 19.

Before long, the bubble stops. The fish men lead you into a musty-smelling underwater city. All the buildings are tentlike structures made of membranes. When you look up, you discover that a ceiling of skin holds the water out of the city.

A woman wearing scaly attire greets you without any sign of friendliness. To your surprise, she speaks English. "Come," she says, "I will show you how to skin a fish."

"Wait a minute!" you interrupt. "Who are you? What are we doing here?"

"It's not important who we are," she snaps. "You are now our slaves."

"How did you learn English?" asks Andrea.

"From the slaves," she replies.

Tony asks, "Did your people ever live above the water?"

The fish woman nods. "Long ago we lived on an island called Atlantis. Now, no more questions. You have work to do."

Turn to page 95.

The extraterrestrials seem to accept your refusal. Then one hands you a pink pill.

"After you swallow this medicine, you will fall asleep for an hour or two. You will awaken on your boat, alone. Your friends are curious about life on another planet so they will be returning to Vaena with us," says the voice in your head.

"How do I know this pill won't hurt me?" you ask suspiciously. "Can you prove that it isn't poisonous?"

"We have no intention of harming you. We only want you to forget about this encounter."

You're not sure you can trust the Vaenatians. You wonder if you could pretend to swallow the pill and fall asleep.

But could you get away with it? The extraterrestrials may have some way of testing to see if you're really asleep. For that matter, they may even know what you're thinking right now!

If you hide the pill under your tongue, turn to page 49.

If you gulp down the medicine, turn to page 84.

After EE721 and NK525 leave, you arrange a pile of pillows in a corner and curl up for a nap. But you can't fall asleep. You feel as if you're being watched. You open one eye and peer at the robots. Is it your imagination or are they really staring at you? You decide to take a closer look.

As you stand up, you slip on a silky pillow and crash against the wall of controls. Red lights flash and motors hum. Ear-splitting beeps fill the room. No sooner do you regain your balance than you find all eleven robots advancing toward you! Their hooklike arms are extended like menacing claws.

There's no place to hide! You'll have to command the robots to stop. You stare in confusion at the controls, then quickly begin turning knobs and flicking switches, hoping to discover the right combination. You are just about to type STOP on the computer keyboard when a robot claw pierces your shoulder.

Despite the incredible pain, you turn to punch and kick the monstrous machines. But you are outnumbered. The androids are twice as big as you, and their strength is beyond that of any human. By the time the two sisters return, you are dead.

The End

You wrap your arms around the brass chest and listen to the voices. You don't know what you'll do if they approach. There is no way you can defend yourself and the trunk is too heavy to drag away. You just have to hope that whoever is on the island won't find you.

All night long, you sit by the treasure chest, trembling every time you hear a voice. You wait anxiously for the first sign of dawn. As you watch the sky turn pink and lavender, you realize no one is speaking anymore. You hear only insects buzzing and waves crashing on the shore. Even though it seems as though you're safe, you decide not to take any chances. You remain right beside the trunk.

Several hours pass before you hear voices again. Please let it be Andrea, you silently plead. The voices *are* approaching this time, and in broad daylight you're sure to be seen. Just as you start to panic, you realize they're calling your name. You stand up and race toward Andrea and the Coast Guard officer with enormous relief.

On the sail home, you forget about the unexplained voices you heard in the night. You and Andrea are too busy discussing what you'll do with the treasure.

The End

The fish woman teaches you to peel the skin off fish, then stretch the membrane on a frame. "Our houses and clothes are made of this skin," she explains.

She takes you to a large tent filled with people skinning fish. The stench is overwhelming. A guard ties each of your ankles to those of the people beside you, then hands you a knife and points to an enormous pile of fish.

As you peel the skin off the slimy fish, you realize you could simply cut the rope around your ankles with the knife. Since the fish woman has left, there is only one guard watching thirty slaves. You and your friends might be able to slip away unnoticed.

But then what? Where would you hide? How would you find your way back to the transportation bubble? You're dying to free yourself immediately, yet maybe you should wait until you can talk with your friends and plan your escape more carefully.

If you think you'd better hold off escaping until you know your way around, turn to page 101.

If you're intent on getting away right now, turn to page 104.

"Please don't go any further," you urge Tony. "I'm afraid something terrible is going to happen."

He shrugs. "Okay, we'll look for wreckage tomorrow."

The three of you sit in the cabin eating the sandwiches you brought from home. You're too nervous to have much of an appetite.

"Pretty weird cheese," comments Tony.

"It tastes more like tuna fish," adds Andrea.

"It was okay when I ate it yesterday," you reply. You take a deep breath, trying to calm yourself. Then it hits you. It's not the cheese that's fishy, it's the air. But why?

"You don't have any dead fish on board, do you, Tony?" you ask.

Before he can answer, you hear a muffled noise on the deck.

"A sea gull?" Andrea suggests.

"No, they were footsteps," you whisper, nearly choking with panic. "Listen!"

Turn to page 103.

You stop thinking about stalling tactics and concentrate on being a model prisoner. Even though your arm is numb and your leg muscles are cramped, you stay perfectly motionless, perfectly silent. When Andrea tries to struggle, you glare at her harshly. Stop it, you signal to her.

Mickey stares at you as he smokes a cigarette. Then he bounds up the stairs. You feel the boat begin to sail. Where is he taking us? you wonder.

Even though you're terrified, you try not to panic. You gaze reassuringly into your friends' eyes. You concentrate on memorizing how Mickey and Shark look so you'll be able to describe them to the Coast Guard—*if* you ever see the Coast Guard again.

You have no idea what time it is when the boat finally stops moving. Mickey ambles downstairs, picks you up, and slings you over his shoulder. It is all you can do not to whimper. Stay calm, you tell yourself, stay calm.

Turn to page 111.

Just then you see two men appear on the deck of the yacht. You try to memorize their faces, but as soon as they see you watching, one of them raises a gun.

You drop to the deck and Tony runs back to the cabin. You hear the yacht's engine start up.

"We'll follow them!" shouts Tony.

"Don't get too close!" you warn him.

The *Louisa* trails behind the yacht for several minutes before Tony shouts, "They're going so fast I may not be able to keep up!"

Suddenly, you hear shooting.

"Are you all right?" you call to Tony.

"It's the Coast Guard!" he cries. "The pirates were racing right toward the Coast Guard ship!" He stops the *Louisa* and both of you watch the Coast Guard overtake the yacht.

Back on land, a Coast Guard officer congratulates you and Tony for helping to catch the dangerous pirate, Mickey Shore, and his brother, Shark. You and Tony grin with pride, but the best part of the day comes when Andrea emerges unharmed from the yacht.

The End

"I'm going to fly the plane a bit lower," you tell Andrea as you steer the plane in yet another circle.

"Is this safe?" she asks. "It's giving me the creeps!"

"I just want to find out if that's Jill," you reply. Beads of perspiration appear on your forehead. You know you shouldn't be flying so low. "Can you see anything more?" you ask.

"Yes," says Andrea. "I think I can see one of the faces. It looks like—"

She never finishes the sentence. An unseen force yanks the plane straight into the ocean! There is no time to think. All you can do is scream as you plunge deeper and deeper into the water.

You feel a horrible wrenching. One wing breaks loose, then the other. All the windows shatter. And slowly, fragments of the plane begin to fall off. You and Andrea clutch each other desperately as the water rushes around you.

The End

You concentrate on observing your surroundings so you'll be able to sneak away some other day. Out of the corner of your eye, you watch Andrea and Tony at work. No one talks at all and you decide you'd better not try to start a conversation with anyone. For endless hours, you strip the scales off dozens of fish.

Finally, at the end of the day, the guard gives you one raw fish for dinner. Yuck! Your appetite vanishes. You have to force yourself to chew the uncooked flesh. While you are eating, the English-speaking woman counts the fish each slave has skinned.

"You are too slow!" she scolds you. "Unless you work faster, I will have to find another use for you."

Since you hate skinning fish, the idea of a different job sounds great. Besides, you'd get to see another part of this underwater city.

Turn to page 106.

As the steps approach the cabin, the fish smell grows more intense. Your heart flutters like a frightened moth. "Tony, call the Coast Guard!" you whisper.

But Tony is motionless with horror. He is the first to see the five fish men enter the cabin.

Although you are terrified, you can't take your eyes off these strange beings. They look like ordinary men except for their tight, shimmering clothes which seem to be made of fish skin! They speak to each other in an unfamiliar language as they grab you and your friends.

You struggle desperately, but the fish men are very powerful. They shove you across the deck into a bubblelike container moored to the side of the *Louisa*. There they tie your hands with a peculiar brown cord. You feel the bubble sink deep into the water, pulling the *Louisa* down with it.

"Where are you taking us?" you ask, dreading the answer.

The fish men just stare at you. They don't understand.

Turn to page 90.

"When the guard turns his back, we cut the cords and run," you murmur to Andrea and Tony.

They nod in agreement.

Unfortunately, the guard is very attentive. Nearly an hour passes before his attention is diverted. When he yells at a slave on the other side of the room, you whisper, "Now!"

The three of you slash the cords around your ankles and slip out of the tent. You lead the way, followed by Andrea and Tony. The blood pounding in your ears nearly drowns out the sound of shouting behind you. Still racing as fast as you can, you glance over your shoulder to see the guard grappling with your friends! You hesitate for a second, but realize there's nothing you can do to help.

You continue running left, then right, then right again through the underwater city. To your dismay, all the fish-skin tents look alike. You're not entirely sure you're really headed toward the transportation bubble.

At the next intersection, you pause, hoping to get a sense of direction. But before you can take a good look at your surroundings, you hear angry shrieks behind you. There's no time to waste now!

You guess you have enough of a head start to run to the bubble without getting caught—if you can find the way. But maybe it's safer to hide for now. You could easily sneak into an unoccupied tent.

*If you continue toward the bubble,
turn to page 68.*

If you look for an empty tent, turn to page 108.

You guide the plane up to normal cruising altitude and head for Miami. Over the radio, you report your sighting to the Coast Guard. Even though it's too soon to be certain, you feel confident that the people you spotted are Jill and her family. You can't help feeling proud of yourself.

As soon as you land the plane, you and Andrea hurry into the airport to phone the Coast Guard.

"I just reported a yellow life raft floating in the Northeast Providence Channel between Eleuthera and Great Abaco Island," you tell the officer. "Can you please tell me who was on that life raft?"

"We have no report on that yet," he tells you. "Call back in an hour or two."

How can you wait that long? Even though the suspense has killed your appetite, you and Andrea try to distract yourselves with a pizza.

When you finally call the Coast Guard back, you are told, "Yes, we have the names of that party in the life raft." You listen carefully as he reads you four unfamiliar names.

It's not Jill's family after all! Your heart sinks. You'll have to resume your search tomorrow.

The End

The next day, you work even more slowly. When the fish woman sees how little you've done, she snaps, "Come, you imbecile." You silently wave good-bye to your friends before following her out of the tent.

As you walk with the fish woman, you try to learn more about her way of life, but she ignores your questions. Finally, by the outer wall of the city, she ties a long rope around your waist and says, "I'm afraid you are good for only one thing."

"What's that?" you ask. For the first time, you wonder if you were better off skinning fish.

"Shark bait," she replies. With a sharp fingernail, she scratches a long cut on your arm. Before you can protest, she shoves you through a spongy passageway into the ocean.

In your panic, you swallow huge mouthfuls of water. You barely notice the stream of blood rising from your arm as you flail about. And you are so terrified that you don't even see the shark until its jaws close around your leg.

The End

You duck inside the first unoccupied tent you find. Unfortunately, there are no closets in which to hide and no furniture to conceal you. You do see a big basket made of dried seaweed. You could curl up inside, but there is no cover. Anyone searching the tent would probably find you.

You hear the crowd approaching. Where else can you hide? There are some things on the floor that look like sleeping bags. Maybe you could crawl into one and pretend to be asleep. After all, except for your clothes, you look just like the inhabitants of this underwater city.

The shouting is right outside the tent. You have to decide immediately!

If you wriggle into a sleeping bag, turn to page 24.

If you climb into the basket, turn to page 43.

The plane seems to fly with a mind of its own. You shield your eyes from the glare and concentrate on everything you love best about life. You think about your family, your friends, and all the fun you've had on the beach. You try to get used to the idea that you may die any minute now.

Gradually, you sense that the intense light is growing dimmer. You peer cautiously between your fingers. Sure enough, the plane has stopped glowing. And the yellow haze has disappeared.

To your relief, all the controls are functioning normally. You discover you are just a few degrees off course. Without a moment's hesitation, you turn the plane and head home. Then you radio in a report of Andrea's evacuation. You hope she's all right.

As soon as you land, you hurry home. You're not sure how to explain what happened. What if people think you're an incompetent pilot? What if they think you made up the whole story?

Turn to page 116.

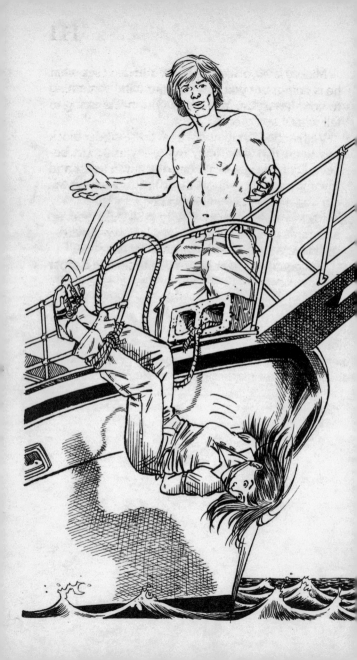

Mickey lays you on the deck. You can't see what he is doing, but you can feel him tying something to your left ankle. You crane your neck, trying to tell what's going on.

With a shudder, you discover that a cinder block has been roped to your leg! All your good behavior got you nothing! You writhe with terror and try to scream, but you just end up choking on the cloth stuffed inside your mouth.

Mickey eyes you scornfully. He picks you up and hurls you and the cinder block overboard.

"Have a nice swim!" he calls cruelly.

But you don't hear him. You are sinking deeper and deeper through the dark water to your death.

The End

As you splash through one last channel, your heart beats faster. The orange shape is a life raft!

"Jill!" you call, letting your hopes run wild.

You can hardly believe your eyes when a figure rises from the life raft and begins to move toward you. It *is* Jill!

"What happened? Are you okay? Where's your family?" You and Andrea both talk at once.

"It was the strangest thing," says Jill as she embraces you. "We were sailing along when suddenly our boat started to rise into the air! We tried to radio for help, but all we got was static. Finally, we jumped off the boat with the life raft. And it's a good thing we did, because our boat disappeared—just evaporated!"

"What about your parents and your brother?" you ask.

Jill points to the life raft. "They're pretty weak, but I think they'll be all right once they have some water."

"I'm so glad you're okay!" you exclaim with relief, and Jill hugs you again.

The End

You're not sure if Mickey calls your parents. Tied up under the deck, you lose track of time. Shark returns, then leaves again. Mickey feeds you peanut-butter sandwiches every now and then, but he won't allow you to talk while you're eating.

There are a million things you want to ask him—Where are we sailing? What are you going to do with us? What happened to the *Louisa?* But you just gobble the sandwiches silently.

One night, the blare of a bullhorn shatters your restless sleep. "Repeat, this is the United States Coast Guard," you hear. "You are surrounded. Do not start the engine or we'll shoot."

Suddenly, you hear the boat's engine roar. Shots ring out, sounding dangerously close.

What if a bullet hits us? you worry. What if the boat sinks? You can't believe you've survived so long only to risk death now that you're being rescued!

Finally, you hear the engine stop. The gunfire abruptly ends. All is quiet. You hold your breath, not knowing what to expect.

Stomp, stomp, stomp.

Someone is coming down the steps. It's too dark to see who it is. You hope that it's not Mickey trying to get rid of you before the Coast Guard boards the boat. You strain your eyes trying to get a glimpse.

The beam of a flashlight darts around the room. In the reflected light, you recognize the Coast Guard uniform! Even before your gags are removed, you, Tony, and Andrea begin to cheer.

The End

114

"I guess I'll visit your brother," you tell NK525. "Maybe I'll be happier on Mars."

The next day you and NK525 begin your journey to Mars. It takes only three days to reach the planet, but a whole week to find her brother, JG816.

You immediately like JG816's easy laugh. He shows you around his camp and talks about the village he and his friends will build. You decide to stay with him. You say good-bye to NK525.

During your first few years on Mars, you help JG816 establish a village. It doesn't look like any place on Earth, but you name the settlement New Miami after your former home. Your village is so successful that it becomes a model for extraplanetary pioneers. More and more people move to Mars until New Miami is no longer a small settlement, but a bustling city. On your twenty-fifth birthday, the citizens of Mars nominate you to be mayor of New Miami.

Turn to page 73.

For the first few months after the mission to Earth departs without you, everything goes very well. You become famous for leading a research expedition to a distant planet in your solar system and you spend many hours celebrating with your Vaenatian friends.

But gradually, you realize that something is wrong. You finally tell Andrea, "Ever since I turned down that trip to Earth, I've been obsessed with curiosity. I wake up in the middle of the night and wonder if the missionaries will manage to prevent the Earthlings from destroying their planet."

"Why do you bother thinking about that?" asks Andrea.

"Because no one has heard a word from the missionaries since they entered Earth's atmosphere!" you reply. "What happened to them? Was there a terrible accident? Or did they discover they preferred living on Earth? Maybe Earth is better than we remember."

"Look," says Andrea, "just forget about it. You can't follow them there alone and even if you could, and you found out what happened, what could you do about it? Nothing."

But you can't forget about it. Day and night you wonder. You can't concentrate on your research. Since you rarely sleep, you're always getting sick. At first, your friends are sympathetic, but they soon grow tired of hearing you babble about the mission to Earth. Before you know what has happened, your life on Vaena is no longer idyllic. In fact, it has become a living nightmare.

The End

After Andrea is rescued and has returned home, she phones you. "Did you call the Federal Aviation Administration?" she asks.

"No," you reply. "I haven't even told my parents."

"We've got to file a report! This is important!" she exclaims. "Tell your parents right now."

Your mother and father are concerned, but you can tell they think you're exaggerating.

"I'll have the plane checked out by a mechanic," says your father. "It sounds like there may have been a short in the electrical system."

You know that wasn't the problem.

The next day, you and Andrea report your bizarre experience to the FAA. A bored clerk listens to your story, then gives you a pile of forms to fill out. As far as you know, no one ever investigates the mysterious yellow haze. But for the rest of your life, you remember what happened.

The End

ABOUT THE AUTHOR

DEBORAH LERME GOODMAN has a BFA in weaving and a graduate degree in museum education. She began writing for children as an education coordinator at the Smithsonian Institution, where her books *The Magic Shuttle* and *Bee Quilting* were published. Ms. Goodman is also the author of *The Throne of Zeus, The Magic of the Unicorn,* and *The Trumpet of Terror* in Bantam's Choose Your Own Adventure series. The author lives in Cambridge, Massachusetts, with her husband, John.

ABOUT THE ILLUSTRATOR

FRANK BOLLE studied at Pratt Institute. He has worked as an illustrator for many national magazines, and now creates and draws cartoons for magazines as well. He has also worked in advertising and children's educational materials, and has drawn and collaborated on several newspaper comic strips, including *Annie*. A native of Brooklyn Heights, New York, Mr. Bolle now works and lives in Westport, Connecticut.

YOUR ULTIMATE CHALLENGE!

 **FROM TENOPIA**

From Edward Packard, Creator of Choose Your Own Adventure® Comes an All-new, Action-packed Adventure Series.

ESCAPE—*You're lost amidst the awesome dangers of the mysterious planet Tenopia. Your only hope is to find the galactic patrol station. Will you make the right decisions? Or will you be trapped forever? There is only one escape!*

☐ **ESCAPE FROM TENOPIA** *BOOK #1: TENOPIA ISLAND The adventure begins when your space pod crashes on Tenopia Island. Look out for the huge man-eating spiders and the weird half-human crogocides. 25472/$2.50*

☐ **ESCAPE FROM TENOPIA** *BOOK #2: TRAPPED IN THE SEA KINGDOM The adventure continues deep beneath the ocean waves in the kingdom of Saleria where a sea storm rages endlessly. Beware of the flesh-eating fish and the underwater pirates. 25473/$2.50*

☐ **ESCAPE FROM TENOPIA** *BOOK #3: TERROR ON KABRAN The galactic patrol is on the continent of Kabran—but the terrain is treacherous beyond your wildest imaginings. Can you make your way to safety? Or are you trapped forever? (On sale in July)*

And there will be four **ESCAPE FROM FROME**™ *books in the fall of 1986.*

Prices and availability subject to change without notice.

Bantam Books, Inc., Dept. ES2, 414 East Golf Road, Des Plaines, Ill. 60016

Please send me the books I have checked above. I am enclosing $_____ (please add $1.50 to cover postage and handling. Send check or money order—no cash or C.O.D.'s please).

Mr/Ms _____

Address _____

City/State _____ Zip _____

ES2—6/86

Please allow four to six weeks for delivery. This offer expires 12/86.

CHOOSE YOUR OWN ADVENTURE

☐	25763	PRISONER OF THE ANT PEOPLE #25	$2.25
☐	25916	THE PHANTOM SUBMARINE #26	$2.25
☐	26309	THE HORROR OF HIGH RIDGE #27	$2.25
☐	26252	MOUNTAIN SURVIVAL #28	$2.25
☐	26308	TROUBLE ON PLANET EARTH #29	$2.25
☐	26374	THE CURSE OF BATTERSLEA HALL #30	$2.25
☐	26185	VAMPIRE EXPRESS #31	$2.25
☐	25764	TREASURE DIVER #32	$2.25
☐	25918	THE DRAGON'S DEN #33	$2.25
☐	24344	THE MYSTERY OF HIGHLAND CREST #34	$1.95
☐	25967	JOURNEY TO STONEHENGE #35	$2.25
☐	24522	THE SECRET TREASURE OF TIBET #36	$1.95
☐	25778	WAR WITH THE EVIL POWER MASTER #37	$2.25
☐	25818	SUPERCOMPUTER #39	$2.25
☐	26265	THE THRONE OF ZEUS #40	$2.25
☐	26062	SEARCH FOR MOUNTAIN GORILLAS #41	$2.25
☐	26313	THE MYSTERY OF ECHO LODGE #42	$2.25
☐	24822	GRAND CANYON ODYSSEY #43	$1.95
☐	24892	THE MYSTERY OF URA SENKE #44	$1.95
☐	24963	YOU ARE A SHARK #45	$1.95
☐	24991	THE DEADLY SHADOW #46	$1.95
☐	25069	OUTLAWS OF SHERWOOD FOREST #47	$1.95
☐	25134	SPY FOR GEORGE WASHINGTON #48	$1.95
☐	25177	DANGER AT ANCHOR MINE #49	$2.25
☐	25296	RETURN TO CAVE OF TIME #50	$2.25
☐	25242	MAGIC OF THE UNICORN #51	$2.25
☐	25488	GHOST HUNTER #52	$2.25
☐	25489	CASE OF THE SILK KING #53	$2.25
☐	25490	FOREST OF FEAR #54	$2.25
☐	25491	TRUMPET OF TERROR #55	$2.25
☐	25861	ENCHANTED KINGDOM #56	$2.25

Prices and availability subject to change without notice.

Bantam Books, Inc., Dept. AV, 414 East Golf Road, Des Plaines, Ill. 60016

Please send me the books I have checked above. I am enclosing $_____
(please add $1.50 to cover postage and handling). Send check or money order
—no cash or C.O.D.'s please.

Mr/Mrs/Miss _____

Address _____

City _____ State/Zip _____

AV—9/86

Please allow four to six weeks for delivery. This offer expires 3/87.